The Shunra and the Schmetterling

YOEL HOFFMANN

Translated from the Hebrew
by Peter Cole

A NEW DIRECTIONS
BOOK

D1262212

The Shunra and the Schmetterling is published by arrangement with the Keter Publishing House and the Harris/Elon Agency of Israel.

Grateful acknowledgment is made to Conjunctions, which first published parts of The Shunra and the Schmetterling.

Design by Semadar Megged
First published as a New Directions Paperbook (NDP980) in 2004
Manufactured in the United States of America.
New Directions Books are printed on acid-free paper.
Published simultaneously in Canada by Penguin Books Canada Limited.

Library of Congress Cataloging-in-Publication Data:
Hoffmann, Yoel.
[Ha-shunra va ha-shmetterling. Hebrew]
The shunra and the schmetterling / by Yoel Hoffmann ; translated from the Hebrew by Peter Cole.
p. cm.
ISBN 0-8112-1567-9 (alk. paper)
I. Cole, Peter. II. Title.
PJ5054.H6319S5815 2004
892.4'36—dc22   2004000950

New Directions Books are published for James Laughlin
by New Directions Publishing Corporation
80 Eighth Avenue, New York 10011

הַשּׁוּנְרָא

The Shunra
and the
Schmetterling

וְהַשְׁמֶעְטֶרְלִינְג

1   **a.**

From oblivion there ascends, like that leg-
endary bird rising from its ashes, the
veranda on which my father's father Isaac
Emerich sat, along with my grandmother
Emma. The veranda of the world itself—
whose heart is an electric lightbulb.
Beside it, on the wall (like Eve, naked
within that X-ray we call the Garden of
Eden) sits a transparent lizard. This is the
veranda on which my grandfather sat and
sent out his hand like Napoleon, looking
across the battlefield toward the villages
of Hayriyya and Saqiyya, when he said to
me in his voice which exists on the right
side of creation entirely—I was a child at

the time—"*Dort ist Arabien.*" (There is the land of the Arabs.)

It is extremely hard to see him stand and go. He is located now in another time, and the air is filled with cordless voices. "*Shavu'a tov*"* is no longer played on the radio.

He sits, dead, within a time that isn't his, and points at a place that no longer exists. Something like the big blocks of ice we would wrap up in a white cloth and put in the bottom drawer of the icebox—or the ball that fell from the school playground onto the back porch—brings that time around like a cosmic loop.

If my grandmother Emma now recited the song of the egg (*kod kod kod kod kod kodaa-sh, minden napra et toyaa-sh*),** time would split open and reveal the time hidden within it, where—preserved in a baking mold—is the scent of potatoes.

---

* "*Have a Good Week*" (Hebrew), a song sung at the end of the Sabbath
** Hungarian children's song

b.

I give my father's father the cat. My father's father releases white butterflies into the space of the home, and the old cat chases them as though in a slow-motion movie. But when a butterfly rises in the air, my grandfather performs an act like that of the one who was crucified, and in his hand he lifts the cat toward the sky of the room, which is fashioned in the form of a ceiling.

On the top floor (the sky's sky), the Heymans are calling in Jewish between the tubs set out for the laundry. If there's a mouse in the worlds-on-high, they say *moyz*,* and I—a child—hear Johann Sebastian Bach on Arlosoroff Street, near Monkey Park, while the *shunra*** *shunra shunra* and the *Schmetterling**** ...

* *mouse (Yiddish)*
** *cat (Aramaic)*
*** *butterfly (German)*

c.

How does one draw a veranda after two thousand years of exile? A broken railing. Grillwork like Auschwitz. A floor laid with the tiles of pogroms, and the Nuremberg laws on the wall's plaster ...

I know. The earth turns like a carousel, and in this revolving everything is rinsed in the air. Autumn yields rain, and spring the fragrance of grass, as in a banal song, and my grandfather—who day after day spread my math notebook open on the table, like a patient's sheets, and wrote the correct digits beside the equal sign for me—diverted the evil winds that blew from school (numbers and the lines of geometry). Someone shattered the great union, and my father's father, who loved me, concealed the sight of fractions from me.

d.

Mr. Tsehayek, who had a grocery store, wandered like the cranes from Baghdad to the Land of Israel.

His golden monocle and gabardine pants, which hindered the movement of the wings, along with the need to look respectable among the cans of peas … all these composed the pure logic of Ramat Gan. What was created wore an exterior such as this and was rounded at the ends, as in the form of Mrs. Zoller, whose name was associated with the health clinic, but whom I saw feeling a peach.

And within all these—the large closet with a mirror inside it, and in that mirror were always reflected, as seas are reflected in the skies above, two bronze beds. On the right side of the mirror was the bed of Isaac Emerich, and on the left side, the bed that belonged to Emma, and the measure of the depth in the picture-reflected was the measure of the depth of outer space.

2   a.

If I want to remember, I remember only in tinted shades, and something like a gull, or gulls.

Childhood, as it recedes, becomes ......er. My mother in her various outlines and my father in his single outline are, trust me, sufficient.

At the cemetery, two marble columns rise up toward the clouds. *There* I grow cannabis plants. Plant after plant, among the remains of flesh and bone.

I remember steps in the sun. A flight of stairs, as they say.

My wife, whose name is Nicola, polishes the mirrors at home. I know, I tell her, where every pot is. Try me.

She does, but I forget one—in which she once made orange marmalade, though the pot is clearly in view.

b.

The sun comes and the sun goes, like a noise on the top floor of the building, where it is not possible to tap on the ceiling with an iron-tipped umbrella or a parasol.

My *raison d'être* you'll have to seek in biology books. *There* the learned explain, like a roofer placing one roof-tile next to another, how I take a silver watch out of my waistcoat pocket.

I remember autumn. My right hand was in the Atlantic. Five fingers on the ocean floor.

Ancient fish surrounded the hand, like extremely religious Jews. The trunk of the arm rising from the depths must have seemed in their eyes—which bulged from their sockets—like a divine revelation.

c.

In that meeting of clear and obscure I grew up.

My grandfather sailed on that Arlosoroff Street veranda, looking across toward Hayriyya and Saqiyya to the place where the ball of earth sailed too, carrying with it the thin layer of air that encircled it, as all of us breathed.

Trees, in a way, were much like lungs. And the upper boughs—where the birds stood still—gave forth the sound of the water they held.

Each tree was an *individuum*. There was the one that "would come home late at night bent over." And the one that "laughed last," and so on.

Butterflies stood at the edge of the eye.

The warning sirens (there were wars then) completed themselves like circles one draws with a compass.

Sometimes stars were doubled by the lesser lights.

There was an upper light and there were lights below, and jackals howled in the great space between the two worlds.

In your mind's eye you could see a man walking from Ramat Gan to Petah Tikvah and being devoured.

d.

My grandfather bent his head because the burden of the memory of women drew him, with the gravity of the pelvis, toward the floor. Like Solomon the king, he ate apple cake at Café Kapulsky next to the Ordea Cinema.

Biblical air surrounded him in his bed with the bronze bars as the angel closed the shutters of my eyes. I dreamed of coins, and he already knew a thing or two and wouldn't even think of suggesting to the pair of mothers that they divide the only infant. He'd have revived the dead baby with the power of thought's idleness.

His death (he missed two breaths) was so peaceful because he knew he was destined to return, deceased, to the streets.

Whoever sees him sees and enters the restaurant or cosmetics store, and no one bothers to say, "I just saw a dead man on the street," since his life walks along beside him.

3   **a.**

My uncle Ladislaus, who was a doctor, received a donkey from the Health Fund.*

At night, the donkey stood on Bialik Street between the stars in the sky and the stars in the sand and brayed like Arkady Dukhin.**

* *instead of a car*
** *popular singer with a coarse voice*

All sorts of women whose names were Hilda tossed in their sleep. A kind of line, like the pale lightning they call a *decree*, descended on Moshe Shertok's* house and it was possible to see the purple flowers of the bougainvillea, though no one looked at them.

The donkey's heart most likely went out toward another donkey, one larger and stripped of all corporeality. At night the divine donkey filled this space, and by day—a man from Vienna whose right hand held a parasol.

b.

The word *fertig*** rolled like thunder between the middle of the night and the hours of the dawn. You know how the sun comes up. A ball made of molten gold, because someone's bare feet have touched the floor.

* Israel's first foreign minister, aka Moshe Sharett
** finished (German)

Imagine a primordial jar of kefir. Before there was "chaos and void." And not a table in the world. Not a single bed. The jar contains no memories, nor does the kefir it holds.

c.

Uncle Ladislaus hung an imaginary violin where one normally hangs up coats and took hold of a razor.

The face he saw in the mirror he silently called the face of morning, but in fact he did not understand the reflection.

Outside, the donkey too gazed at the inner reflection, and each of them saw behind his world. It is extremely hard to rescue time from these sights, which freeze like the subtle vapors given off by ice a moment before the movement begins.

You can see the Argaman* factory just like

* here the name of the factory, but also a sensuous purple (Hebrew)

in love poems by Ibn Gabirol. How that
colorful fabric emerges from the machin-
ery. Or those long cords that are stretched
and woven at the Yerushalmi plant beside
the Yarkon.**

d.

Mr. Katchko is already standing by the
flower pots on the porch, waiting for my
Uncle Ladislaus to come out and go to the
donkey.

The white parasol Uncle Ladislaus is
holding in his right hand teaches Mr.
Katchko that even the Trade Union of
Hebrew Workers flies through the air.
Uncle Ladislaus's stethoscope amplifies
the sound of the Messiah's footsteps.

And I haven't yet spoken of the beads of
dew in the lower world. Of Mr. Katchko's
daughter who has angina. But Uncle
Ladislaus lets nature run its course and
simply wiggles the muscles of his ears

** *a river in Tel Aviv*

until she laughs, though her throat is full
of phlegm.

When it comes to the wild doves that
came to me (the great miracle of my childhood), a healing power moves through all
ten of my fingers and the sun rises toward
the zenith (or toward the nadir, as they
say).

4   **a.**

If I could sing to my mother as Allen
Ginsberg sang to his, I would. *Yisgadal
veyisqadash,* * like that, which is one of the
too-late additions to that great book, the
beginning of which is In the beginning.

Her name. The dead babies she gave
birth to like a blind typesetter who brings
to light combinations of letters according
to the smell of the lead.

Her going toward death like a carpen-
ter into an old piece of furniture he'd

* *The beginning of the Kaddish, the Jewish prayer of mourning:
"Magnified and sanctified [be His great name throughout the
world]"*

carved and planed without looking back
even once.

b.

At the oil press of dreams, she removes
her white apron and I can see she's a very
thin woman. A blind cat is chasing me,
and I have a hard time asking her: Was the
birth difficult? And what time is it *now*?

Take the Maccabees, and the elephant
from the history book, and rise, rise, rise
dead woman if only you'd left us at least a
neck.

Explain the air. The rain. The movement
of my mouth when I speak and the pecu-
liar appearance of other people amassed as
though at a Quaker meeting the length
and breadth of this flat plain mouthing
complex words such as "if" or "or,"
though there's nothing to say before these
sights: skies, and other skies that are
wrapped within them, and the stars are all
gathered toward the interior.

c.

I give your dresses names:
Dress One, or the dress of distant goats.
A dress made of plaids that are white and
red.
One could call it the dress of the café table.
A transparent dress whose number is
Seven, or Eight.
A dress whose name is "the last one," and
in which one could still discern the many
bodies of yours that it held.

Or I could list the parts of the body: Leg.
Leg. A foot. The place beneath the arms
we call *pits*. The walls of the heart. Pores or
maybe not. Hair. Or maybe also not. Ten
toes of the foot until the soul gives out and
all the rest as in Pompeii, where only the
paintings on the wall remained: a woman
bathing, with a kingfisher over her head.

5   **a.**

I can tell you of the many windows I saw

after you died. Six, six, and in every window—the child Avremaleh and his mother feeding him from a large spoon that she brought from Theresienstadt. And a mulberry tree in the yard, and under the tree there were kittens, and even Mr. Reimalt (the General Zionists' honorable delegate) had a walk-on part upon this stage, which grew distant from you, like the celestial bodies.

I also saw Mrs. Yoel, who hid a bottle of raspberry concentrate at the back of the pantry. Up and down the length of Rav Kook Street, she alone said "Hambursh," (when she spoke of Hamburg). There was something, mother, reminiscent of an umbrella about her pelvis, and because the Germans hunted attorneys' wives, who grew wide from the waist on down, she did well to sail with the winds of time.

b.

I also saw the tailor who had sewn, from his foot on up, eternal trousers.

A large transparency came through the Singer sewing machine, which stood in the middle of the store like an ancient altar for the offerings of man: on the wall hung pieces of unfinished suits, and people went behind the curtain and took off their clothes. What was the tailor's name? Everyone I could ask is dead.

("Schneider, Schneider, *kim aroys,*"* we might call to him, as one calls out to a snail in its shell, and he'll emerge from his store waving a ruler.)

c.

In those days there were seven days to the week.

The first day was the day of the wild pigeon. From the child Hannan's house, countless wild pigeons streamed whose color was the color of wine. These ancient sons of men the size of turtle doves wandered from tree to tree, an upper sea of

---

* *come out (Yiddish), as in a children's song*

wild pigeons, as though the soul of the earth were floating on air.

The second day was the day of the crow. This is the crow created from within the days of my childhood and into the history books overhead, and it called out—for me alone—the unutterable name of God. The third day was the day of ebb and flow. I could see the heart of the cloud in the upper waters coming and going. The fourth day was the day of tremendous sleep. The two sides of time were gathered to the middle until they were cancelled. Its other name was the day of the great equilibrium.

The fifth day was the day that the sun grew clear, and it wore the face of the moon until the end of the sixth day, which was the final day of the counting of the fowl and the celestial bodies—the day that came before.

The Sabbath was the day of my life, because on that day, masculine and feminine, I was spun by two guinea pigs whose eyes were like black buttons and whose wisdom was deeper than the infinite number of days.

d.

I know that you lived on like a shadow
within my living father, in the full length
of his figure, and when he spread his arms
wide, one was whiter than the other, as on
the telephone, when he said the name
"Andreas" and the end of the word disap-
peared.

All sorts of signs, like sirens, taught
me that your death evolved into my life, in
an act of kindness and grace, because it
was not possible to absorb these three letters* without mediation.

6   a.

My father wore the crow suit of Mondays,
despite the hot winds from the East.

From within his walking to the insur-
ance company at the corner of Allenby, I

---

* I-m-a, mother (Hebrew)

recall gray legends: partially paralyzed princes placed an LP on the gramophone. The outer surface of the world (neckties and BBC broadcasts) was set free.

A man came from out of the blue and suddenly said, "My name is Rivkin." Stories were concocted as one installs a window frame and places the glass pane within it, then opens it, and shuts it, even though it was all transparent from the start.

In the book *Between the Grass and the Stars*,* a young man named Heaven loves a young woman whose name is Forfend, in the grove next to Sheikh Munis, where the chain of my Raleigh bicycle slipped out of the gears, and I saw, through the thin metal rods called spokes, Rachel Sirotta among the myrtles.

b.

If I could take off like a light plane, I would. Already there was evening and the

* *a collection of Hebrew children's stories from the '40s*

moon in the Ayalon Valley, and the sun over Gibeon; these were ordinary phenomena in those days, like the new Hebrew, which brought forth tulips.

What could I have done, with my singularity so very clear, as clear as it was at the moment of creation.

It's extremely hard to remember how the chain got back onto the teeth of the gears, because there are wonders greater still. I saw my face in the water and how that face had come to appear, and also the motion of the arm, which I had to watch out for—because who knows what might be hanging from it.

We didn't realize then that within us there lies another person dying to get out, though someone had already seen to it that we knew the formula for salicylic acid and the caloric value of an egg. But what difference does it make, Rachel Sirotta—Galileo's climbing to the top of a tower to throw objects off of it?

c.

On the way from Sheikh Munis, we saw a
praying mantis. The mantis was standing
on a clump of weeds, alone, like a muezzin
who had forgotten his lines. We were four
or five, and Ehud Kaplan, who two years
later wrapped himself up in cotton and
burned, raised the mantis and placed the
creature on the front light of his bike, and
when we got to Ramat Gan, the praying
mantis was standing on the light, magnified and sanctified be his great name—
Yisgadal veyisqadash shemei rabbah.

7   **a.**

In Rachel Sirotta's kitchen the water is
boiling. Her father and mother are filling
the top ten percent of the room, and their
heads are in Izmir. Oy! How the sun has
sunk.

The birds call out names such as Erzurum and Erzurum and Erzurum, until Rachel Sirotta conceives of a fine composition and draws a pansy at the edge of the page. She can't include the sun in the work but writes out the word.

And the word horse, or the words a white horse, though she doesn't know how the property of whiteness takes part in the horse's being.

There is no space without time, but there is time without space in Rachel Sirotta's composition, which she is writing, I reflected, and no one knows where that reflection is.

And within all this, stretched across the work, a sky and small cloud like the hand of a man, and nouns carefully rounded, and all the punctuation marks in their proper places.

b.

Mr. Sirotta remembers the journey east.

The train stood in the field of corn, and suddenly the air was filled with fire-

flies. Strange, Mr. Sirotta thinks, since the
sun was shining.

c.

Another sight: Muslims falling on their
faces.

Another sight: The train comes in a
cloud, and the cloud is made of another
cloud, and so on and so forth until the
innermost heart is revealed.

There he is caught in the riddle of
Who remembers the one who remembers?—and the answer is amazingly sim-
ple, but he doesn't remember it, because
of the great waters (and this is *the place*
that is in his dream and time: *Hosh'ana
Raba*).*

And all the while (if while is a word) his
wife was steeping tea, and maybe the
vapor rising was the source of the cloud
and the mystery is found in the other

* *literally, the great appeal (Aramaic): the seventh day of the
Feast of Tabernacles*

thing, which is called (like something reflected on its own) a *kum-kum*.*

8   a.

In those days they didn't speak on phones that were not connected by wires, and the wires linked those who spoke, although they were under the ground.

The receivers were larger, and sometimes looked like soup bowls. Winds blew from every direction, and there were signs, as when the moon stood still.

We didn't yet know the meaning of the words *ifkha mistabra,** and therefore the streets were flooded with light and the bicycle repairman, the homosexual, also inherited the earth.

We were able to take off from the construction planks in the empty lots. Before

* *kettle (Hebrew)*
** *the opposite holds (Aramaic)*

the feature films they would show car-
toons of Mickey Mouse, and the radio
spoke of a man whose name was
Megsaisai.

Maybe we were on the backs of large
birds of passage, as the schools were
upside down.

b.

Oy! When we sang *"Adon 'Olam"** in the
morning on the corner of Rav Kook and
Diamond Street.

Beterem kol yetzir nivra** we said, and
the teacher Shoshana Wein, who was a
creature since she came to us after the
Creation, called the roll name by name,
and everyone said: Present.

Sometimes the clouds passed toward
the slope of Rav Kook Street and onward
at times from there to Ramat Yitzhak, and
sometimes, like an answer to the prayer

* *a hymn in the Hebrew liturgy*
** *a line from this hymn, "before any creature was created"*

"*Adon 'Olam*," the sun rose from the police station.

From his bedroom Mr. Krinitzi* gazed at the children and thought to himself that he too had been a child and now his eyes are called *those that look out.***
From all over the world they brought clocks to Palestina in order to solve the riddle of time, and they'd already begun to sit in cafés, but we ran from place to place as though time were pressing.

c.

I remember things such as the sliding door and the great snow of 1950.
There was a camel-man in the back yard. A kind of dinosaur who looked out of broken windows and cast a spell.
And we saw the teacher Shoshana's panties. The rainbow in the sky testified to the fact that all sorts of fateful things were occurring. We ate the notebooks, and

* *the first mayor of Ramat Gan*
** *Ecclesiastes 12:3*

whatever we were told to learn by heart we knew (oh, we knew) from the end to the start, and the meaning we flew like kites.

9 a.

In those days a female whale accompanied me.

The lights flashed and I saw that the room—couch and all—had been replaced by the interior chamber of the female whale (ribs and all, like the look of another chamber) and though I was within it, the good eye gazed at me.

The landscapes I saw were the Land of Ohnor: The teacher, Aharon White-Sheep, who brought with him his inflamed ear. The vice-principal Avgad Fisch, a frightening man whose back was bent over from reading the notes that children passed back and forth in secret, and especially my stepmother Mathilda, whom the kitchen towels urged on, sail by sail, toward the fields of Kukurutz.

Imagine, for a moment, a life in which I am on deck calling out Albert, Albert, because Albert is passing by—for this after all is the meaning of civilization: this movement of people from place to place, opticians among them as well.

b.

I remember how my father Andreas married Mathilda.

All day long Mathilda sliced bread and spread butter until the sandwiches filled the space of the soul of the large mammal. Mr. Yaar, who had a speech impediment, was there and also Mathilda's friends, the visitors Gertrude and Gertrude.

My father Andreas leaned, pale, against the ribs of the whale, and in his hand he held a 33 1/3 record of *Iphigenia at Aulis.*

The rabbi spoke to the giant in the sky. He said:

You see that I am old and my bent knees are what I am, and you examine the inward parts and the heart along the paths of your thunder.

Bestow upon this land abundance of goodness and evil. The train of your red dress as the sun sets, and the great yellow in the morning—oh, my heart's delight. Even a worm like me, awash in desire, French women, etc., has in his heart pity for this woman Mathilda, the daughter of Rabbi Avraham of Frankfurt, and for this slanting man Andreas, the son of Yitzhak, and I lay before you this plea, this prayer, that you do with them as you did with the small (violet bluish) flower that's called the Chalice of Sharon.

c.

In those days I said *yud heh* (instead of *tet vav*),* and in summer I weeded at Bacharach's nursery.

* 15 *in Hebrew numerology; yud (ten) and heh (five) are the first two letters of the unpronounceable name of God (YUD-HEH-VUV-HEH) and are therefore normally replaced by tet (nine) and vav (six).*

Gertrude and Gertrude explained the universe to one another. On the porch, an apple cake served as proof. My stepmother passed by the doorways.

Something like a distant noise was trapped in the walls of the home. The air, as it were, refuted things: the movement of peoples from place to place. Electric engines. Indications of distance. Each of these concealed something else.

My father Andreas knew these secrets because something blue trailed behind him. Something blue.

10   a.

Sometimes the sky stretched out as though it contained sixty suns.

This was the year of Dina Issachar, whose algebra notebooks looked like well-plowed fields. How we saw the movie *Ben-Hur* on a CinemaScope screen and the Roman chariots raced straight toward us.

Amid the din and tumult of the horses'

whinnying and the rattling of swords, you placed your left hand with the bitten fingernails and gold, heart-shaped ring on the armrest, and on it I placed a hand which, if it was mine, I didn't know it at the time because of the greatness of the moment when the wheels of the chariot spun within one another and grooves were formed.

b.

Afterward we walked up Bialik Street, from Ramah and up to Kofer HaYishuv, and the magic of the movie house gave way to spells of another sort.

We saw a double image of the two of us in the display window of Moshe Eliyahu Office Supplies. The reflection was doubled in another mirror, or a mirror's reflection, then doubled again. A great wind spun the street signs, and when the rain came we took cover in the stairwell of the health clinic, and from there we saw the fire that was lit in the sky.

(And what we promised then, as the rain rose from the ground and returned to its place, you surely remember now as well, in Ramat HaSharon, half a century later, with your husband who sketches electrical poles on paper, and we had already set them up, already then, along the length of the world)

c.

That year we also sang "*The Internationale.*"

We didn't know what "starvelings"* were but we saw a man who was so tall that his neck was bent forward and the back of his head extended, as it were, along the length of the ceiling. We tested our powers with difficult words like Popocatepetl (and didn't know it was the name of a male mountain that watches over the beauty sleep of his beloved, who is dressed in a gown of snow—the female mountain).

* *"Arise, starvelings, from your slumber"—the first line of "The Internationale"*

How is it possible to describe such a spring? A butterfly big as a volume of Talmud stood above our heads.

11 a.

It's a wonder that a man carries his bones wherever he goes. English teachers especially, because of the letter *s*, which one has to add to the verb in the third person present and everyone forgets.

b.

It is extremely difficult to raise the moon. Avgad Fisch does what he can (press-ups and so forth) but sometimes the moon, particularly when it's in its lesser phases, gets stuck on something and stops.

c.

"I believe that life is an error," Andreas my father says to himself. On nights like these he hears the music of Bruckner. In the next room, on the other side of the wall, Gertrude is sitting (Gertrude is sick in bed) and Mathilda is sitting and Hugo and his wife Yolanda are sitting and Franz is sitting.

d.

... Franz is about to say something. Perhaps he already has and Hugo's wife is speaking. Hugo raises his hand and stops Franz. (First Yolanda will speak!) Franz removes his eyeglasses and tosses them onto the table. Later he gets up and goes, and as he turns to the hallway his body is emptied and he starts (perhaps as a result of the insult) to fly.

e.

At ten the moon rights itself and stands in its usual place.

Andreas my father goes to the window, and in the other room my stepmother

Mathilda goes to the window too. Franz (in the hallway) takes his coat off the hanger and turns the pockets inside out.

12 a.

That morning Avgad Fisch confiscates a condom (like the Zeppelin that exploded and human beings fell between the burning cracks to the ground). The school is already tilting to one side like a nightcap.

If I were a poet I would sing the new day of Aharon White-Sheep and the line of prophets he is leading (like Selma Lagerlöf's wild geese) to class 8-B.

I know. We have done what was wrong in the eyes of God (and have even uttered the unpronounceable letters of His name). We were happy when the wife of the math teacher died (because the test was cancelled). But the water we drank from the faucet was inner water and our hands drew signs in the air.

b.

What were we talking about? The wonder is that we were talking.

Here, here, we said so they'd throw us a ball, and the ball, like planets one sees at the planetarium, came near and moved away.

We had names like Shimon Danishevsky, and we leaned—each with his name, between two kiosks, both of which contained an Iraqi man and a mountain of mocha and vanilla wafers—against the iron railings.

From the shards of memories it's extremely hard to reconstruct a picture of the world. Once someone shouted: Pinyeh. Pinyeh.*

c.

I can *make* faces or *conceal* faces because history is like a geyser.

* a man's name

I know that ships dropped anchor at Ordea Square and were moored to the edge of the sidewalk. We heard the horn from the direction of Bialik Street, and when the huge prow passed by the Town Hall, we knew that the masts would follow soon.

(True. Not everyone saw. But Haya Shenholtz, whom everyone said would "give," saw. And Sha'ul Aslan, whose father sold peanuts, saw as well)

13   a.

To Mathilda's *Kaffeeklatsches* Gertrude comes once again with Gertrude, and Hugo who grinds his teeth comes, and so does his wife Yolanda.

Sometimes the moon is broken and Franz (who sits with Andreas my father and listens to Bruckner's music) fixes it with tremendous compassion.

b.

My father Andreas has a kettle of his own,
and he steeps tea—though his room turns
(through the power of Bruckner's music)
into a valley of vision.

The wood of the crucifixion is there
and there too is Pontius Pilate, and among
the rabble the apostles as well.

c.

The work of repair is extremely hard.
Sometimes a cup cracks or someone (in
the other room) formulates a thought to
himself.

Principally Hugo's wife speaks. How
on the way from Ramot HaShavim
etcetera etcetera ... And at the same time
(near my father) the son of God is bound
to the cross.

d.

Franz draws an arc in the air.

Then he rolls his eyeballs three or four times. This movement of his—which duplicates the movement of the heavenly bodies—summons all sorts of powers that lie beyond the window.

The painting of the woods on the wall is inverted now, but because the lights come from below, this world too is correct, though the crown turns toward the heart of the earth and the roots are exposed.

14   a.

On Passover we slept on tables at the Luria School, and we stole Nehemiah's eyeglasses.

In the morning Nehemiah looked out to Mount Meron and most likely saw the primary matter before there was light and before the waters were gathered. We didn't return the glasses to him because one

of the lenses fell out of the frame and
therefore Nehemiah stood, like the bird
known as the kiwi, at Tel Hai,* in front of
the roaring lion and cried.

b.

Later we went as far as Nebi Yosha' and
from there we saw Mount Hermon and
the lakes. (I think we went out of shame.
We were no longer little and not yet big,
and had brought with us hard-boiled eggs
from home.)

At night the girls laughed amongst themselves as though they knew something. A
bird (maybe a cockatoo) called: *Ouk. Ouk.*

c.

The floor of the sky was exposed, and it

---

* *burial site of Joseph Trumpeldor, a national hero who was killed
defending the settlement by this name; a statue of a lion marks
the grave.*

was as though the divine chef had spilled, from among the thousands of trays that he carries, nuggets of gold.

The world was like a large woman—an alcoholic—wearing a black dress, her body adorned with all her jewelry. Or that the mind had emerged from the skull and presented itself in such colors.

d.

In the morning we went up to the edge of the cliff and stood there, our backs to the chasm. The wind picked up. Trees bowed down to the ground. Avgad Fisch came before us and, like that prophet who destroyed the prophets of Ba'al,* his sleeves flapping, shouted:

Bassan!
Berkovitz!
Gu'eta!
Gross!

* I Kings 18:19–40

Goralnik!
Hefetz!
Hakhamov!
Idel!
Marciano!
Papernik!
Qadosh!* ...

On the way back to Tiberias, *en passant* as
they say, we saw a barber. He was sitting
on the chair, by himself, and before him
was a large mirror: Ohana (or Farjun)
among countless possibilities.

1^5 a.

Andreas my father and Franz see now
what is hidden behind the surface of
things. Pillars of fire that suddenly rise up
from the street. Writing on the wall. If
they say a word such as *sjadu,*** the butterfly effect occurs.

---

* *Holy (Hebrew), also a family name*
** *see (Icelandic)*

My father takes a step (to the side) and
Franz takes two (forward) and neverthe-
less one does not catch up with the other
or lag behind him.

b.

At Café Maʻayan (where they are sitting)
there sits a woman as well, who com-
plains: And I said ... and she said ... and I
said ... and she said ... until it becomes
clear that she (that is, the woman at Café
Maʻayan) is right.

Franz sends his hand out toward the
west and almost by chance pulls down the
sun.

(aetla eitthvert annad, my father says, hun
virdist)*

c.

Franz says: If there were a condition in the

* Icelandic, but the author has forgotten what it means

world, that one needs to start from the first thing—where would we start from?

My father says: Perhaps from the body?

Franz says: Yes, but look what a waste that would be (two eyes and so forth).

My father says: If so, one has to start from nothing.

Franz says: Right. (And to Mrs. Ma'ayan:) Tea.

d.

Mrs. Ma'ayan's large dog (an English sheepdog) comes and one immediately sees that both sides (left and right) are required. Their biographies (Franz's and Andreas my father's) are bound up in each other and the moon comes out.

16   a.

At midnight, Andreas my father takes off the black coat and goes to the bedroom.

First he wants to turn on the light, but when he sees the silver color of the sheets and the shadow that comes and goes, he is startled.

b.

He leans against the doorframe and says: I have already seen this sight. Very thin butterflies and a cloud's reflection on ice. What is the meaning of the words *daud eiginkona* (dead woman) if one cancels out the other?

Just then Mathilda emerges from the bed sheets and stands in the dreamy light like an elephant participating in mysterious rites.

Andreas, she says, Andreas, what happened?

c.

In the morning, Andreas my father takes a cup from the cupboard and sits staring at

it, waiting for the Flanders farmers paint-
ed on its surface to wave their pitchforks.

A bulb of who-knows-how-many-
watts is lit in the sky.

17   a.

We saw a million stalks (how they rise in
the pristine air as though the forces of
gravity didn't exist).

We saw the great humanity of the
winged creatures that wander like Mon-
gols on the backs of transparent horses, in
formations that Euclid saw only in his
dreams.

And amidst all this they told us the letters
ba-ga-d-ke-fa-t and so on ...,* as though
someone needed to cough at this concert
or count (one by one) the sounds.

In the morning we came and they
showed us—on the blackboard—all sorts
of shapes.

* *a mnemonic pertaining to the correct pronunciation of soft and
hard consonants in Hebrew*

b.

They gave names to the mountains and cut them out on paper like slices of a wedding cake.

They said to us *meneh** (*mene tekel upharsin*)** and we counted the continents and seas and rivers like a warehouse clerk or a peddler standing on a market corner.

Then they took the wavy forms of the horizon and straightened them out and told us to measure angles.

(And each time, as in a horror movie where they stop for ads for crock-pots or cleaning fluid, they made us go out for recess.)

c.

We went in and went out and went in and went out when the electric bell rang

---

* count (Hebrew)
** the cryptic Aramaic inscription on the Babylonian palace wall that Daniel alone was able to interpret (Daniel 5:25)

and they didn't tell us about the antelopes.

For we could have sat in the classroom and said *hey* (or *here*) whenever they leapt and made that movement with the fingers of our hands or waited quietly (like Rahamim Gu'eta who brought a lizard to school and the lizard stared at the board) until the lesson was over.

d.

I remember one thing in particular: Aharon White-Sheep says *"they shall repair the breaches of the house"** and Yamima Hefetz raises her hand.

Aharon White-Sheep died the day they landed on the moon. Yamima Hefetz got married and divorced and married again and went from Ramat Gan to Rana'ana and from there she went to Michigan in the United States and came back to Dizengoff Street where again she waved the hand she'd waved then and said "home repairs."

* *II Kings 12:6, referring to the Temple in Jerusalem*

18 a.

An English widow sells books on Bialik Street, and Andreas my father follows her and looks at the books.

The widow Sassoo-n waves a bamboo stalk with feathers at its end and tears through cobwebs. My father takes a step, and the widow Sassoo-n takes two, and suddenly a great wave of sunshine strikes the storefront window and enfolds the widow Sassoo-n like a chunk of amber.

b.

And though she is trapped in the congealed light the widow Sassoo-n speaks:

On the upper storey of this world is a place where people drink tea (and she too drinks it she says) and one need only extend the arms to that place and take the porcelain ear between a finger and thumb and leave the remaining three fingers suspended in the air.

My father thinks: Some of the books speak of the nature of things and some of the things of nature.

He extends his arms from one end of the store to the other, above the datebooks and adding machines, and touches the body of the widow Sassoo-n.

(The meaning of this motion becomes clear in a book by Heidegger, and from the other books there emerge the flowers of the Land of Israel and rare birds fly up.

Archeology books spread before them a royal mosaic and the astrologers scatter new suns across the ceiling)

c.

But as in a realistic story, a bus passes on Bialik Street and the gust of wind rattles the newspaper stand.

Impossible worlds are relegated to the compartments of the imagination, and Andreas my father sees (with the eyes of his spirit) extremely vulgar sights.

19   a.

Sometimes Mathilda hears the neighing of horses and it seems to her that she too can flick her withers.

In the summer, swarms of flies burst into her house and Mathilda hangs a strip from the ceiling light, and the flies come to it until it comes to resemble those trains of death.

b.

The summer is her spring.

She sends colorful postcards to all sorts of places around the world and scatters things generously. When people come to ask for money, she says my husband gave at the office, but she sees what others do not—a blotch on the sun. Clocks that have stopped, and so forth.

She sketches maps and sets Andreas my father in different locations. He is standing beside a waterfall and she moves the

tigers to the west. He is standing atop a
mountain and she is shaking off snow.

Though not on purpose she crushes
pieces of history underfoot, and after-
wards Zionist Congresses have to be fixed
and all sorts of other things as well.

d.

When Gertrude and Gertrude come (in
the afternoon) her strength is tripled and
she paves new paths in flower gardens
also, directly toward the fine stems of the
orchids.

Each one of them (she herself and
Gertrude and Gertrude) turns from the
center in which things are what they are
(soap = soap, and so on) toward the more
distant periphery and disseminates,
almost unintentionally, the gospel truth.

("Ulrich said," one of them says, for
example, and reports what Ulrich said)

As though in accordance with the law of
the level of water, we fell from school to
school and in each place the chairs became
larger and the desk became larger (and
this information is, in the end, a matter for
the government).

The teacher Mattityahu is reading
from Goethe's *Faust,* and where Gretchen
speaks she constricts her voice. *Faust*
seeks happiness in all sorts of ways, and he
finds it at recess.

And again the sun (an old friend),
which always comes at the same fixed
time for our meeting at the zenith.

b.

Girls now have bras, and cotton under-
pants have been replaced by silk.

The school is full of naked bodies (if
one subtracts the clothes from the sum
total) and sometimes, when there's an
assembly and everyone is gathered inside

the gymnasium, apocalyptic visions take
shape (on account of the myriad limbs).

c.

They taught us the difference between
objective and subjective.

This is what they said: Objective is the
shadow a sick man casts on the carpet
between the hours of five and six, in
November. Subjective is the need to sleep,
or the sick man remembered a year later.

They left us alone in this search, and
therefore we discovered the great bird that
stands between the heaven and earth, at
the place where the line of sight returns.

d.

Like, for example, someone we called the
bear because his spine was bowed by the
weight of his head, which was carried
close to the table between the imaginary
eye on the right and the imaginary eye on
the left.

We knew that he was a single human unit and would go into the army (and that we would go), and if we were on the passive side of Mercy perhaps we would step on a street corner sometime near a fur goods store.

21   **a.**

Behind the bear sat the foreigner, who had already played basketball on all sorts of courts, and when he looked in the blackboard's direction it was as though he saw another homeland.

Teachers (such as Sesna'i, who taught social studies) walked around him as one walks around a totem.

b.

Once, the foreigner spoke. He parted his lips and plucked the chords of his throat, and you could hear that he said *"shalosh,"** but no one knew what the question was that went with this answer.

(I think about water, fire, and air. But then dust has to go … and who knows on what courts he plays now and where the question has gone since then)

c.

We looked everywhere for the Shunammite and the clear-eyed one.
   We looked for them among the flocks of people that moved about in the schoolyard like imperial penguins, and we looked for them under the window of the physics lab.
   What a refined mechanism these two were: one who would wave her braids, and the other who saw everything upside down.

* three (Hebrew)

d.

See how they speak to one another.

The Shunammite says: Yesterday, you know which waist-belt I'm talking about, the red one whose color is the color of that liquid.

The clear-eyed one says: Yes, and the lips match, and the cloth beneath, you know the one that the white worms spit out of their mouths.

And the Shunammite says: These are the two feet, you know, and what covers them is called a shoe, and it is the hour (without speaking of hands on the watch) when the ball that is always burning touches the sea.

22   a.

In those days Andreas my father studied sounds.

He took a stone in his hand and with it

he struck walls, drainpipes, storefront windows, sewer covers.

Ramat Gan spread out greatly and in his eyes came to resemble a tremendous xylophone.

On Rav Kook Street they built the new health clinic (there my father produced a G) and on Bialik Street they added a bank (C) and an office building (B-flat). These and the more muted sounds of the elements, which are very hard to incorporate into the known scales (such as the sound of lightning).

b.

Sometimes, on the brink of madness, it seems he is looking for Franz in a strange courtyard and a toothless woman shows him the way.

He finds Franz asleep, but now he can already fly. He takes Franz's down quilt and carries it up to the ceiling, and from there he looks down at Franz like a bug.

c.

Franz knew, or didn't know, about the matter of these dreams. But whether he knew or not he is now battling the seasons.

When spring comes he sets a large picture of winter before him, and thus he delays it considerably, and when summer arrives he sets before himself a picture of fall, and hurries it along until the end of the one blends into the start of the other.

d.

Sanity is an extremely polite word, and if they'd asked Mathilda she would not even have known it existed.

For Mathilda, these are the days of cabbage soup. How she perfected it! Her ways with cabbage soup knew no bounds.

23 **a.**

Sometimes the bell rang and a person we did not know stood in the doorway. I am so and so he said and have no hand. But he *had* a hand.

Or he said, allow me to introduce myself, and he pointed to himself.

b.

They bring the person who pointed to himself into the hall, a place where coats are hung.

(This standing in the hallway, as people point to themselves, is supported by tremendous powers: fire that is red at the center and other very distant bodies)

c.

Such as, for instance, when the person whose name is Hosea came and spoke:

I am Hosea (so he said). It would seem at first that the air is clear but in fact the world is full of particles of earth called dust, and they hover in the space of a home like spray that rises up from a waterfall.

And there is (so he said) an apparatus that inhales the dust ...

Or the person whose name is Lipkin, who stood by the coats and said, Katz sent me, and you could see (in your mind's eye) how Katz is sending him and he goes and Katz stands there watching.

24   **a.**

On *hamsin** nights Mathilda lay like the pyramids at Giza and waited, but Andreas my father was busy reckoning the end.

The end of the comet that fell to earth in Siberia and knocked over forests, as

---

* *the warm seasonal wind from the desert*

toothpicks are knocked over in jackstraw.
The end of the soup from which vapors
rise toward the kitchen ceiling, and the
end of first names when he says "Franz"
and sprays the "z."

b.

Parallel to Mathilda's belly he too had a
belly, and he bore his belly as one bears a
huge cross down the Via Dolorosa of the
hallway between the kitchen and the bathroom.

(His belly too was called Andreas, but
it was Andreas the belly, whereas he—was
Andreas the father)

c.

In the morning Mathilda rose like
Zimmerman to his copper pipes.

My father Andreas sought to celebrate
the new day. Light came through the
panes of glass and there were sounds.
Suddenly the number five seemed to him

entirely logical and he raised the fingers of his hand like someone holding an owl in one hand and a mirror in the other. (*Lehayeikhon lehayeikhon** he said)

2⁵   a.

The sun came up like a yellow parachute and held us by fine threads so we would not fall into the depths of the earth.

Andreas my father walked west down Rav Kook Street, and I rode an old bike by the candy factory and the Galei-Gil pool.

In front of the pole with the shifting colors I saw Sesna'i, the teacher, inside his car, a Contessa. Here I was I, at that point in spacetime, and here he was he, and the two of us stood in the reddish light and all around was Zion.

* *"to your life" (Aramaic), which combines behayeikhon (during your life—from the Kaddish: "May He establish His kingdom during your life and during your days") and le'hayyim (to life)*

b.

Where were they leading me, those pieces
of rubber known as pedals?

As in a movie by Woody Allen I rode
twenty or thirty meters above the ground,
while everyone rolled up their pants, like
one does before going to Nahal*, and said
words such as "dialectical materialism."

From my air machine I saw the Polish
and German immigrants explaining life to
themselves like a mangy dog.

c.

On one side of the intersection was Mrs.
Asherov's house and on the other there
stood, like the cricket in Bialik's poem, a
lonely whore.

At the place where the diamond
exchange stands today, she lay on the
ground, and if the arrow of time is vertical
(and what is in the present has already

* an army unit with a socialist tradition

been), a bounty of crystal rose from her, to
a height of thirty floors.

26   a.

Now final exams are already near and
we've written dates on our palms.

We copied this information into
sheaves of government paper, and all the
while we saw the late-May sky being cut
into window-sized pieces.

(On this day, despite the extreme cau-
tion we were ordered to take regarding all
things relating to the order of the world,
fish flew through the air)

b.

When we left, we threw our ballpoint
pens onto the roof of the bicycle hut and
went to the beach at the end of Gordon
Street, where the wind blew from every
direction.

We grasped racquets in our hands and white balls, and God— whom they'd concealed from us— swelled like a giant balloon.

Summer vacation began with Mrs. Steinholtz, whom we'd seen on the warm sand wearing a bathing suit checkered like a table of logarithms.

c.

By evening the sun stood at the end of the sea and a freighter sailed toward it.

Crows spoke like people who knew a thing or two, and the medusas glowed at the beach like lights in the park.

We thought of people on the other side of the earth, and how no one falls as it turns and turns. And the great ball of fire goes there and stands over their heads and tomorrow, amazingly enough, it will come once again from the East to Tel Aviv.

27 a.

July was extremely hot, and therefore we saw American movies in places called David's Palace and so forth. We waited with people of Romanian extraction for the doors to open and meanwhile looked at the pictures in the lobby.

b.

On the Sabbath we went to Seven Mills and rented a boat.

Shimon Danishevsky, who'd studied metalwork at Max Fine,* rowed out to the opening to the sea. There he put down the oars, and we sat in that bathtub made of wood, between the city and the wide water, and from our fingernails created dragonflies.

---

* a vocational school

c.

The baking powder was called, I believe, Arditi, and the girls, who had matured considerably, were (for the most part) Nitza.

We thought principally about two things:

The great nakedness everyone had come together to cover—and which we'd seen in the movie *Bitter Rice*—and Martin Heidegger.

d.

The man who sold hummus on Bialik Street taught us the secret of hypnosis.

He raised his eyes to the ceiling as though he saw Baghdad there with all its minarets, and meanwhile the sun came through the letters O R I E N T A L R E S T A U R A N T and established itself in the space of the shop, which was—on the whole—a kind of crystal ball.

The new light washed the familiar

worlds to the street, and Um Kulthum came to us from within the kitchen like a great wave of sleep.

28 a.

Andreas my father tosses books into a large bush, and the books turn yellow in the heat of the sun and curl as though fire were rising out of the earth and licking them.

(The words "nimbus clouds" disturb him greatly. He does not agree with the word nimbus.)

b.

The bush stands next to the wall of Mrs. Twersky's house, and when she looks out the window the skeletons of the books make her chin blush and she thinks within this framework: Here is Ramat Gan,

where trees burst into flower, and never-
theless my daughter has gone to Rhodesia.

c.

At night the moon stands over the head of
Andreas my father.

He wants to depart from what he is
and meanwhile writes "Y-H-V-H"* on the
display windows of a store for electric
appliances.

(Kum-kum? he asks Franz)

d.

In order to annoy the street, he steps more
to the right than the left. His right foot he
names (secretly) "The Widow."

These are the final months of his life,
and only now does he hear, for the very
first time, the word *shwarma*.

* the letters in God's unpronounceable name (Tetragrammaton)

29   a.

It's already the end of August, and never-
theless a donkey comes into the courtyard
and everyone stands there and stares at it.

The donkey is clearly descended from
a line of kings. But now there stand
around him refugees from Hungary,
Germany, and Iraq—and Lermontov,
whose wife was killed in the Italian bom-
bardment, says: "Give him some water.
Give him some water."

b.

Things are doubled in the donkey's eye,
and it's possible to see in them an Austin
Mini Minor and cypress trees and a strip
of sky.

The way to the trash cans is blocked,
and therefore Mrs. Twersky goes there
from the other side of the world.

c.

And as the days of rationing are behind us, Mrs. Yoel has already taken out to the porch her bottle of raspberry concentrate, and she sits among the philodendron plants as she once sat in Hamburg during the thirties.

Today is the last day of August, and tomorrow is September, *v'leit maan defalig*.*

30 **a.**

All sorts of dreams set sail that month.

There were stars outside and *Stars Outside*** by Natan Alterman, and we didn't know the difference between upper and lower.

(You could see scenes that took place only

* *and no one disputes it (Aramaic)*
** *a highly influential book of mid-century modernist Hebrew poems*

once every thousands of years, such as, for example, one man standing in front of another and saying: Schwartz?)

b.

The world had walls. Alas!

Night after night lit what it lit, and Andreas my father was still within it.

Cities like Irkutzk came very close, and we read all sorts of things in the almanac.

c.

Among the names of September there was also the name Miriam Bauer.

Miriam for the *mr* (like *mir* for instance) or the great sea (*yam*), and Bauer because of the ineluctable.

You could hear that people said (when they spoke about bikes) phrases like "I carried her on the handlebars."

31 **a.**

It is very hard to gather memories from
that month, apart from the bit about the
pajamas. Because we were "about to go
into the army," we wore pajamas made of
pure silk.

Taking power from an imaginary line,
we arranged our fingers until our hands
turned into large fans and we could parade
before the mirror like Madame Butterfly:

b.

- *Hast du zwei Hände?*
  (Do you have two hands?)
- *Du hast.*
  (You do.)
- *Hast du zwei Füsse?*
  (Do you have two feet?)
- *Du hast.*
  (You do.)
- *Hast du ein einziges Auge?*
  (Do you have a single eye?)

- *Du hast.*
  (You do.)
- *Hast du noch ein einziges Auge?*
  (Do you have another single eye?)
- *Du hast.*
  (You do.)
- *Sind deine Füsse ganz alleine?*
  (Are your legs all alone?)
- *Ja.*
  (Yes.)
- *Sind deine Hände ganz alleine?*
  (Are your hands all alone?)
- *Ja.*
  (Yes.)
- *Was sehen deine Augen?*
  (What do your eyes see?)
- *Nichts.*
  (Nothing.)

32 a.

Andreas my father is speaking:
In a little while (he says) you will go to another place, and it's good you should

know that your mother loved you. This love (he said) is like a white towel.

Most likely "The Widow" was bothering him, and therefore he lifted it with his two hands and set it on the footrest.

b.

At the beginning (he said) we had nothing but ourselves. Me myself, and your mother (who wore a blue dress) herself. Nothing can explain how it is that *you* came into the space of the world (he said *Weltraum*).

He took hold of "The Widow" with his two hands and removed it from the footrest. Then he went to the gramophone and placed the *St. Matthew's Passion* on it and heard (as one shatters a large aquarium) the voices of the Passion's choir.

33   a.

Franz's coat of many colors is in fact
(*eigentlich*) only a shirt. But because Franz
approaches against-the-sun, as it were,
this shirt—upon which black lines have
been drawn—extends to the nadir.

The question "what" rises again between
Franz and Andreas my father. They get to
the root of things. If one was silent, an
entire hemisphere—like a bird with just
one wing—was forgotten.

b.

Because of death my father speaks in foreign tongues:

Ja, aber meine Tante ...
or: *hayakatta!*
or: *je me lave*

("I wash.") Franz answers to the extent
that he's able, but his capability is limited

because there is in the speech of Andreas
my father a kind of urgency such as, for
example, when he reels off a list of kings,
but not in historical order.

c.

Sometimes his thoughts grow clear and he
says:
  Not that you are not Franz and not
that I am not Andreas. But see how, in the
end, we have no need for this talk.
  Though another question disturbs his
rest. Didn't I once own (he asks) a red
necktie?

34 **a.**

That year, after the month of Adar came
another month of Adar.*
  The scents of that month are beyond
comprehension: Shiraz and Mohar and

* *The Hebrew leap year adds a second month of Adar*

Cannelon went through the space of the world like a tornado.

At the summits of mountains scouts stood and with semaphore flags signaled the movements of the great fish.

According to the Chinese calendar that was a lucky year. Company by company we went (Yehoyakhin carried my rifle, and I pushed Meshullam Abramson) from Beit Dras to Gezer* and back.

b.

Beneath the huge boilers that Staff Sergeant Gantz set afire, we washed the body on the right and the body on the left, though we knew not a thing about the Sefirot.**

We said *tsafra tava**** because three of us ran into a mine and rested for a moment midair.

* a forty kilometer march, each way
** in Kabbalah, emanations of the Godhead
*** Good morning! (Aramaic)

(The Aramaic mediated between the
Hebrew and nothingness)

c.

We loved an imaginary woman (of
Yugoslavian descent).

We said to her (as in a Hollywood
movie) that we were going to war, and we
asked her to sit beside the window and
knit until wool filled the house and spilled
(like that porridge) into the market
square.

In the end, we said, we'll return and
the old dog will recognize us.

d.

The sun rose and after it the moon came
up and the sun went down. Two colossal
males, one of which is active and the other
passive—and I could have raised my hand
and spun the sun dizzy around itself with
a movement of the finger, but this I did
not do.

(Each night the moon came and stood
over our heads like the big rock in
Magritte's painting)

35   a.

Meshullam Abramson (whom I pushed
on the journey from Beit Dras to Gezer
and back) saw visions.

The fields beyond the barbed-wire
fence and the houses of Be'er Tuvia, all
these became in his eyes Armageddon: a
terrible killing field in which we all were
lying, dead.

(We all knew that he suffered since the
sign of the world was Meshullam, and
butterflies which were Meshullam flew
over the tents and a Meshullam whose
color was like the color of morning was
stretched from end to end)

b.

And it's impossible to forget Ora, who
stood behind the fence and waited for
Shimon Danishevsky to come and undo
her bra (the two small metal hooks).

Ora came and went, and she was clearly holy, as freckles covered her face. In the
six times she came, she stood there seven
times and the blouses she wore are memo-
rable as Ben-Gurion's voice in the Tel
Aviv Museum or the brown hull of the
Altalena.*

c.

Anyway. These were the finest days of our
lives. We lay among the huge sheets of
canvas, our shoes beneath the iron bed,
like the roots they dig up in China or
Korea and which possess life-giving prop-
erties although they're all contorted.

---

* a ship that carried arms for the right-wing Jewish underground
in 1948—sunk by the Israeli Army, under Ben-Gurion's
direction.

How *did we think?* By means of association. If, for example, we saw a lizard, a carburetor came to mind.

36   a.

In the fall of that year my stepmother got rid of the twenty-two volumes of the *Brockhaus Encyclopedia,* which she put out in the street.

The twentieth volume with the word *Tod* (death) inside it lies before the tailor's shop, and he turns the wheel of the Singer sewing machine and the wheel that he turns in turn turns another (which is connected to it by a leather strip) and these two wheels drive the great wheel within which move the stars.

b.

In my dead father's room the turntable gathers dust and the records (33 1/3) wobble.

Mathilda's shadow falls on the beds

when she walks from the phone to the bathroom, and from there into the kitchen.

Sometimes Gertrude and Gertrude come, and Hugo from Ramot HaShavim comes, along with his wife Yolanda. And as they pass in front of my father Andreas's room, they lose their third dimension, that is, the quality of depth.

(The sounds of German in the hallway are heard like a concert of music stands.)

c.

Mrs. Yoel died as well and was buried.

They slid her wide pelvis and trove of memories (some of which took on the shape of sights) into the ground and waited to see if the sun (as the philosopher had it) would rise.

Meanwhile, a new generation of wild doves perched on the antenna. And who knows, maybe one of them was called Zavdi'el.

37   a.

From among those days I remember Monica the hairdresser, half of whose face the dentist froze.

When Monica left the clinic on Ro'eh Street 15, there was already a half-moon in the sky and the gravitational force that raised the water of the sea drew her head upward as well until her hair was, as it were, caught in the heavenly gears.

b.

Monica lifted a hand (I remember the polished fingernails, which kept electrical poles in the air) and at seven o'clock in the evening said: *Really!*

Then she turned down Yahalom Street and next to Mr. Gabison's travel agency stopped and looked at the picture of the palm trees.

The pain now had started to return to half of her face, and it was clear that it stood on its own and bore no resemblance to the remainder of things, such as, for example, that I was standing there (my heart and its chambers).

c.

Beyond the glass, behind the palm trees, Mr. Gabison was talking on the phone. Such and such and such and such, and in all probability he'd begun with the creation of the world. The debt that remained, there had been a trip, and into suitcases they had stuffed a dead man's handkerchiefs, and the suitcases went to the wrong airport and were returned.

And further, that the flights leave on time but the great bird sometimes creaks and cracks form along its aluminum body, and through them blue air can be seen and at night black air speckled with gold.

d.

At roughly seven-thirty Gabison turned

off the electricity that lit up the palms and the model plane.

We could see that Mr. Gabison was bent over and how is it that divine man, who is like a tree, can be broken?

Nonetheless it is impossible not to think today that in one way or another he emanated Monica from behind the glass and emanated me who was standing there facing her back, for day after day we turn to him during the morning prayer, saying Gabison. Gabison. (No?)

38   a.

When Monica took off her dress grass-hoppers leapt in the grass.

At the open-air movie theater at Gan Avraham they were showing an American film, and it's entirely possible that the grasshoppers leapt onto Rock Hudson's giant face.

(From where we were lying only the sound could be heard and the light that rose off the screen was like a lower-level lightning)

b.

I saw the place from which the baby emerges. Here it is March, and I love Monica (I thought).

Someone (maybe Monica) cried and other sounds (such as the sounds of shots at the movie theater) and maybe the sound of the grass growing or the voices of my heart and its chambers …

When Monica put the dress back on it was already another day. The weeds had grown a great deal, and you could see (as in a Chagall painting) a cow in the sky.

c.

In the morning. At Mathilda's house. I heard water dripping.

The drops came out of the faucet's tap and very gradually turned to beads until the metal could no longer support their weight and released them into the sink. The sun rose like a sail, and you could hear the sound of the great body creaking.

Ostensibly it was a morning in the month of March. But in fact, in fact what?

1998 April

Today I humble myself before the sky, for no one knows if the great body that stands above the sea is a sun or a moon, and green or verdigris covers the hills.

There is the man whose name now escapes me and there are dreams.

Light comes and light goes as at a train station, when an Indian with a turban comes and rolls a cigarette then climbs aboard a train and the train departs, and you look for him on the bench where he sat, and by the board listing the trains, and you scream in your heart Where art thou Where art thou until you no longer know the meaning of these words. If you ask people they'll tell you they've seen

such an Indian only in pictures but what
do they know.

Now it is already April, two years before
the end of the millennium, and God is
too much revealed. You go into the super-
market and find him in the matzah meal.
You wheel the cart to the aisle with the
chocolate and the jars of honey and
beneath the broken neon lights you read:
Yad Mordechai.* Yad Mordechai. Yad
Mordechai ...

Forty years have passed since Monica said
with a half-frozen face (the 's' she pro-
nounced 'sh') "*shilshul temidi.*"** Now
that her head (and who knows where that
is) has gone white, I understand:

After April May will come, and the large
beetles of May will ascend from the
ground like heavy bombers.

* *the name of the Kibbutz that produced the honey (Hebrew)*
** *chronic diarrhea, instead of permanent wave—a perm
(Hebrew)*